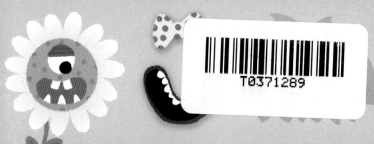

MONSTER FACES
STICKER BOOK

Designed by
Krysia Ellis

Words by
Sam Smith

Stick on the missing eyes to see what these monsters look like.

2

3

4

Select stickers to complete
these spooky characters.

5

Add alien features to finish
these space monsters.

6

7

Choose mouths and noses
for these monsters.

8

Use the stickers to finish these grisly swamp beasts

10

11

Add the eyes and mouths missing from these monster mugshots.

MONSTER I.D. 76486119
MR. SNOOK

MONSTER I.D. 25415673
ZAPPERGEIST

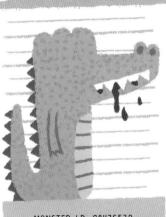

MONSTER I.D. 98476520
CROCOCHOPS

MONSTER I.D. 46280912
ARCTIC PHANTOM

MONSTER I.D. 56379982

THE BIG OOZY

MONSTER I.D. 68462436

CREEPY CRAWLER

MONSTER I.D. 35806512

RAZOR FANG

14

Stick on eyes, mouths and fins to finish these monsters of the deep.

15

Add the finishing touches to
these monsters' party outfits.

16

18

Stick on features to finish
these gruesome monsters.

19

Add arms, legs and mouths to complete these lively monsters.

20

21

22

Use the stickers to complete
these bloodthirsty critters.

Add bolts and facial features to Frankenstein's monster.

First published in 2019 by Usborne Publishing Ltd., Usborne House, 83-85 Saffron Hill, London EC1N 8RT, England. www.usborne.com Copyright © 2019 Usborne Publishing Ltd. The name Usborne and the devices ♀ ♡ are Trade Marks of Usborne Publishing Ltd. All rights reserved. No part of this publication may be reproduced, stored in a retrieval system or transmitted in any form or by any means, electronic, mechanical, photocopying, recording or otherwise without the prior permission of the publisher. Printed in China. UE.